SAFARI PUG

The Dog Who Walked on the Wild Side

LAURA JAMES

Illustrated by ÉGLANTINE CEULEMANS

BLOOMSBURY
LONDON OXFORD NEW YORK NEW DELHI SYDNEY

Bloomsbury Publishing, London, Oxford, New York, New Delhi and Sydney

First published in Great Britain in November 2017 by Bloomsbury Publishing Plc
50 Bedford Square, London WC1B 3DP

www.bloomsbury.com

BLOOMSBURY is a registered trademark of Bloomsbury Publishing Plc

A CIP catalogue record for this book is available from the British Library

ISBN 978 1 4088 6640 5

All papers used by Bloomsbury Publishing are natural, recyclable products made
from wood grown in well managed forests. The manufacturing processes
conform to the environmental regulations of the country of origin

Printed in China by Leo Paper Products, Heshan, Guangdong

1 3 5 7 9 10 8 6 4 2

For Lady Eliza

Chapter 1

It was midnight at No. 10, The Crescent. Pug was sound asleep at the foot of the bed when a loud scream woke him.

'Aaaaargh!'

It was Lady Miranda. She was sitting bolt upright.

'Puuuuug!'

Pug rushed over to her and tilted his head in enquiry.

'Pug, there's a lion in the bedroom!'

A lion?

This was worrying. Pug was glad Lady Miranda had warned him.

Wendy, Lady Miranda's housekeeper, came hurrying into the room.

'Whatever's the matter, m'lady?' she asked.

The sight of Wendy comforted Pug.

'There's a lion, Wendy. A lion!' Lady Miranda insisted, lifting her eye mask.

Pug wondered how she could tell there was a lion in the room with it on. *She must use her nose*, he decided.

'Oh dear, m'lady. Where's he hiding?' asked Wendy.

'There! Over there!' Lady Miranda pointed to her very large wardrobe.

Crumbs! thought Pug. *How did he get in there?*

Wendy took a look.

'He's not in here, m'lady.'

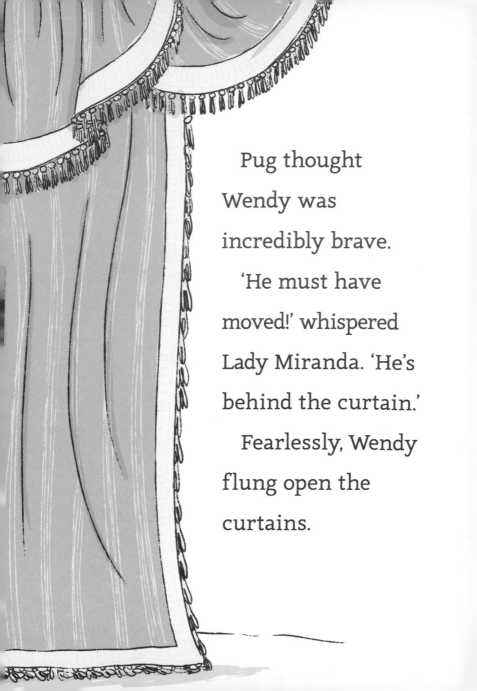

Pug thought Wendy was incredibly brave.

'He must have moved!' whispered Lady Miranda. 'He's behind the curtain.'

Fearlessly, Wendy flung open the curtains.

No lion.

'He's under the bed!' screamed Lady Miranda.

He certainly was a quick mover, this lion.

Lady Miranda hugged Pug for comfort. Pug started to shake. He'd never met a lion before and, judging by Lady Miranda's reaction, he didn't want to.

Wendy went to check under the bed. It took her a while, her knees not being what they once were.

'There's no lion, but there's a lot of crumbs under this bed,' she said, looking at Pug. 'I wonder how they got there.'

Pug hid his head under the blanket.

'Never mind about the crumbs,' said Lady Miranda. 'Where's the lion?'

'I suspect . . .' began Wendy.

'Yes, Wendy?'

'I suspect you were having a nightmare.'

'So we're not in danger of being eaten?'

'Not tonight,' said Wendy, reassuringly. 'But I'll stand guard outside, just in case. Will that be all, m'lady?'

'Yes, thank you, Wendy. Pug's easily scared, you see.'

Wendy nodded. 'Goodnight, m'lady,' she said. 'Night-night, Pug.'

Pug gave a little wag from under the blanket.

'Pug,' whispered Lady Miranda as she put her eye mask back on, 'we need to show Wendy you're not a scaredy-cat.'

Pug wriggled round and rested his head next to hers on the pillow.

'Tomorrow, Pug, you're going to meet a lion.'

Chapter 2

Pug didn't sleep a wink. His hopes that Lady Miranda would forget about him meeting a lion were dashed when Wendy came in with the breakfast tray. Something about the way Wendy opened the curtains seemed to jolt Lady Miranda's memory.

'Wendy,' said Lady Miranda, sitting up in bed. 'Ask Running Footman Will and Running Footmen Liam to have the sedan chair made ready. Please pack the camera, the binoculars and a picnic. We're going on safari. Pug wants to meet a lion!'

Pug ducked back under the covers. It took a lot of persuading to get Pug into the sedan chair but eventually Running Footman Will, Running Footman Liam, Pug and Lady Miranda were off.

The footmen were especially speedy that morning and, much to Lady Miranda's delight, they were first in the queue at the safari park.

As they approached the ticket booth Lady Miranda leaned out of the sedan chair.

'Four tickets for the lion enclosure, please.'

'You can't go into the lion enclosure in that thing!' the ticket lady said, pointing at the sedan chair.

'Why not?' asked Lady Miranda.

'It's not a car,' said the ticket lady. 'The lions are free range in the enclosure. They'll have you for lunch in that flimsy old thing.'

Pug gulped.

'It's not a flimsy old thing!' responded Lady Miranda. 'Besides, Running Footman Will and Running Footman Liam are super-fast and they hardly ever break down.'

'I'm sure they are very fast and very reliable,' said the ticket lady, 'but they're not as fast as a pride of lions.'

'I bet they are!' said Lady Miranda.

The ticket lady was about to accept that bet and give Lady Miranda the tickets when the park supervisor appeared and she decided not to.

'Perhaps,' she said instead, 'you'd like to see our Animal Adventure Land?'

'But Pug wants to meet a lion,' protested Lady Miranda.

'That's simply not possible,' said the ticket lady.

'How about the rhino enclosure?'

'No,' said the ticket lady firmly.

'What about the cheetahs? They look sweet.'

'They're even faster than the lions!' exclaimed the ticket lady, running out of patience. 'And they're not as sweet as they look. I'm afraid the only tickets I can sell you, if you insist on driving that thing,' she said, pointing to the sedan chair, 'are for the Animal Adventure Land. There are some very cute penguins there, and the shop sells lovely home-made ice cream.'

'I have always liked penguins,' mused Lady Miranda.

The footmen nodded encouragingly. Pug wagged his tail. He'd always liked ice cream.

Lady Miranda had a think.

Beep beep!

A car horn interrupted her thoughts. A large queue of traffic had formed behind them.

'Hurry up!' shouted a mean-looking woman in a big car.

'Oh my goodness, that's Arlene von Bling!' exclaimed the ticket lady. 'This must be my lucky day. I can't believe I'm going to meet Arlene von Bling. Does my hair look OK?'

'It looks lovely,' said Lady Mi... The footmen agreed.

Arlene von Bling beeped her horn again.

'She's much grumpier in real life,' said Running Footman Liam, who was afraid Arlene von Bling was going to run him over.

'Who is she?' asked Lady Miranda.

'She's on the telly. Don't you recognise her?' asked the ticket lady.

'I don't watch telly,' replied Lady Miranda.

'Well, she's very famous. She knows everything there is to know about antiques and curiosities. I'm going to ask for her autograph.'

Beep beep!

Woof! Woof! Pug replied.

WOOF!
WOOF!

'Please may I have four tickets to the Animal Adventure Land?' said Lady Miranda, who had finally made her mind up.

'Good choice,' replied the ticket lady.

They took a quick group photograph to celebrate Lady Miranda's excellent decision-making and as Arlene von Bling revved her engine they headed off to the Animal Adventure Land.

Chapter 3

Pug had never seen so many different types of animals all in one place. There were sloths and porcupines, monkeys, and even an armadillo. It was quite smelly and noisy, but there weren't any lions in sight so Pug didn't mind.

They headed straight for the Penguin Kingdom. It was feeding time.

Pug was about to offer the penguins some of Wendy's picnic but the penguin keeper came along with a bucket of fish. This was the penguins' preferred lunch, apparently.

Pug sniffed the bucket.

Yuck!

It was so disgusting that he fell backwards and the entire colony of penguins waddled over him.

Lady Miranda took a photo. 'I knew you'd like penguins,' she said to him as she scooped him up. 'That's precisely why I chose to come here.'

\

'I said you could feed them, but don't pick them up!' came an unexpected shout from the penguin keeper.

'This is Pug, not a penguin,' said Lady Miranda.

'Not you, miss,' he replied. 'I was talking to the lady behind you.'

It was Arlene von Bling.

'I was just moving it off my expensive shoes,' Arlene von Bling muttered, putting the penguin back on the ground and wiping her hands in disgust.

Pug could tell she wasn't really an animal person. He wondered why she'd come to the safari park at all.

* * *

By noon, Running Footman Will, Running Footman Liam, Lady Miranda and Pug found themselves in the depths of the jungle. Lost.

Lady Miranda got the binoculars out. She couldn't see a thing.

Running Footman Will handed her a handkerchief. The binoculars hadn't been used in a while. He gave them a good clean.

As soon as she looked through them again, two heads popped up in front of her.

Pug thought they looked funny.

'Gosh! What are they?' Lady Miranda asked.

'Meerkats,' said Running Footman Will, reading a helpful sign.

Pug padded over to them and they started a game of chase. Lady Miranda got the camera out.

The meerkats were very popular and drew a big crowd. Pug was having fun until an unfortunately loud grumble from his tummy frightened the meerkats away. Lady Miranda decided it was time to eat.

They found some clever footprints on the ground that showed them to the exit. Pug worried they might belong to lions.

It was tricky getting the four of them and the sedan chair through the exit but they were managing quite nicely until Arlene von Bling, who seemed to be in a big hurry, tried to squeeze through too. The man in charge of meerkats came over to see if he could help.

'Perhaps you'd like to step aside,' he said to her. 'It won't take a moment for this party to go through, and then it'll be your turn.'

Pug could see that Arlene von Bling was very cross. As he watched he was amazed to see her bag move all of its own accord, like it was alive.

'*Woof!*' he barked.

'Hang on a second,' exclaimed the meerkat keeper. 'You have our Gladys in your bag!'

It was true. She did.

'Well, how on earth did that get in there?' Arlene von Bling asked innocently.

'Cheeky little scamps,' said the meerkat keeper, with a chuckle. 'They get everywhere. You nearly ended up taking her home. Let's just put her back, shall we?' He placed the meerkat carefully on the ground and she dashed over to the safety of her friends.

Pug wrinkled his brow. There was something about Arlene von Bling he didn't like.

Chapter 4

L ady Miranda found them the perfect spot at the aquarium to eat their lunch.

Pug loved Wendy's picnics.

Lady Miranda was just passing round the sandwiches when Arlene von Bling came charging towards them with a monkey climbing all over her.

Pug took cover.

Seeing Lady Miranda, the monkey jumped into her arms.

Lady Miranda laughed and began feeding him some fruit.

Pug often jumped into Lady Miranda's arms when he got scared. He looked at Arlene von Bling suspiciously.

At that moment the monkey's keeper arrived.

'You've . . . found . . . him!' he said. He was a little out of breath.

'He's quite safe,' Lady Miranda assured him.

'I've a good mind to sue you,' spluttered Arlene von Bling. 'That animal nearly killed me!'

'We're terribly sorry,' said the keeper, recognising Arlene von Bling from the television. 'I've no idea how he managed to escape.'

He switched
on his walkie-
talkie.

'Charlie's been
found,' he said. 'But upset VIP
customers. Code red. Suggest secret
weapon. Over.'

Pug's eyes got bigger. Secret
weapon! What did that mean?

'What's your secret weapon?' asked
Lady Miranda.

'Florence, our lion,' he replied. 'The lion keeper will be along shortly.'

'You're going to feed us to a lion?!'

Pug looked to Lady Miranda nervously.

'No, of course not!' the keeper laughed. 'Florence is our white lion cub. '

'Does she bite?' asked Lady Miranda.

'She's very gentle.'

'Oh, well, in that case,' said Lady

Miranda. 'Pug would like to meet her very much. Wouldn't you, Pug?'

Pug wasn't sure.

When the lion keeper arrived they were shown into the Education Suite at the back of the aquarium. She unlocked the door with a big set of keys. Arlene von Bling took a seat away from the group. It was clear she didn't want to make friends.

'I'd like to introduce you to Florence,' said the lion keeper. 'She's a very rare white lion cub who was born at our safari park.' She opened the crate.

'You go first, Pug,' said Lady Miranda, pushing him towards Florence. 'He can be such a scaredy-cat,' she informed the lion keeper.

Pug remembered how bad Lady Miranda's nightmare had been and peeked gingerly into the darkness.

Two blue eyes blinked back at him. He took a small step closer and waited. Suddenly a big paw came through the bars and bopped him!

He fell over, tummy in the air.

'She likes to play,' said the lion keeper, lifting Florence out of the crate and putting her on the ground next to Pug.

Immediately she pounced and landed on Pug's soft upturned belly. The impact made Pug burp. She jumped off, confused.

Pug sat up quickly. He was nose to nose with a lion! He couldn't believe his own bravery. She was the most beautiful thing Pug had ever seen (apart from Lady Miranda, of course).

Florence gave Pug a big lick across his face.

'She likes him,' said the lion keeper.

'She won't eat him, will she?' asked Lady Miranda.

'Don't worry, Florence prefers milk to pugs,' the lion keeper assured her.

'You say they're rare,' said Arlene von Bling. 'How rare? Are they very valuable?'

They'd all forgotten Arlene von Bling was in the room.

'How much do you think you could sell one for?' she continued.

'Florence isn't for sale,' said the lion keeper, taken aback. 'Besides, she's priceless.'

'So's Pug,' said Lady Miranda. 'And I wouldn't ever sell him either.'

Pug wagged his tail. This was good to hear.

'Well, isn't that nice,' said Arlene von Bling, but her face looked all twisted and mean and Pug didn't believe what she said one bit.

Pug moved away from her and instead listened carefully to the lion keeper as she told them all about Florence. But Florence had other plans. She crouched down and pounced on Pug again, pushing them both under the chairs. Pug scrambled to his feet and tried running away but Florence sped after him.

The ticket lady was right, thought Pug. *Lions are very quick.*

As Florence ran towards Pug a hand swooped down and grabbed her by the scruff of the neck.

The hand belonged to Arlene von Bling.

She lifted Florence into the air. In a moment of quick thinking, Pug grabbed hold of Florence's tail to pull her back, but it was no good.

Arlene von Bling was much

stronger than Pug and she shoved them both into her enormous bag.

Lady Miranda noticed it had gone quiet. 'Where's Pug?' she asked.

'And where's Florence?' asked the lion keeper.

'I've got them,' said Arlene von Bling, brandishing the keys to the Education Suite. 'And you're not having them back! I'll have sold them before sundown. Two for the price of one!' With a wicked laugh she marched out and locked the door behind her.

Lady Miranda, the Running Footmen and the lion keeper were trapped.

Chapter 5

'**P**uuuuug!' screamed Lady Miranda, banging on the door.

'Florence!' shouted the lion keeper, almost as white as the lion herself.

Running Footman Will tried to find a way out.

'It's OK,' said the lion keeper, gathering her senses and reaching for her walkie-talkie. 'I can call for help.'

'Hurry,' said Lady Miranda. 'She mustn't sell Pug!'

* * *

It was dark and a bit of a squish inside Arlene von Bling's bag. Pug did his best to see out. He was sure that Lady Miranda would already be on her way to rescue them but, just in case, he tried his best to think what to do.

He wanted to wriggle out of the bag, but Arlene von Bling's running was very bumpy and Florence wouldn't follow him. He tried pulling her out with his teeth but as he stuck his bottom out of the bag Arlene von Bling elbowed him back in. They were trapped.

As soon as Lady Miranda was set free from the Education Suite, she sprang into action. She and the footmen headed straight to the play area. Lady Miranda had noticed that it had a fort. They climbed to the top of it and got the binoculars out.

Lady Miranda scanned the crowds. It was difficult, but eventually her eyes fell on the lone figure of Arlene von Bling with her bag.

She was taking the most direct route out of the safari park and heading straight for the lion enclosure!

Finally the bumping stopped and Pug and Florence peered out of the bag.

Arlene von Bling was standing next to a really high fence. She started to climb but her pointy shoes and enormous bag were making it difficult.

Then suddenly Pug and Florence felt themselves flying through the air.

Arlene von Bling had thrown them over the fence!

Pug was terrified. He waited for the horrible landing but instead they started swinging gently.

The strap of Arlene von Bling's bag had become caught on the branch of a tree.

Pug and Florence looked out.

It was a long way down.

Arlene von Bling was climbing down the other side of the fence. She had nearly reached the bottom.

Pug barked at her but much to his surprise it seemed to come out as a . . .

Pacing below them was a very angry-looking lion. It was Florence's mother.

Arlene von Bling rapidly began to climb back up the fence as the rest of the pride of lions drew near.

Florence wanted her mother. She gave Pug one last lick, then climbed out of the bag and down the trunk of the tree. Pug looked on anxiously, but he needn't have worried: Florence was a natural climber.

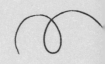

Pug hung precariously from the tree whilst the lions circled underneath. They looked very hungry. Some of them were trying to climb the fence to get a closer look at Arlene von Bling. She threw one of her pointy shoes at them in disgust.

Pug was just hoping that Florence was telling them that pugs don't really taste nice when, unexpectedly, the bag started to slip . . . !

Chapter 6

Beep beep!

Pug looked down. In the nick of time, speeding towards him, came Lady Miranda, standing on top of one of the safari vehicles.

'Jump, Pug, jump!' she shouted as they screeched to a halt under the tree. Running Footman Will and Running Footman Liam tried to distract the circling lions with the leftovers from Wendy's picnic.

Pug was surrounded. He couldn't even see Florence any more. She was lost amongst the bigger lions.

Then Pug looked at Lady Miranda. He'd known she would come to rescue him.

The bag slipped again. It was now hanging from the tiniest tip of the branch. He was running out of time. Pug scrambled out of the bag, shut his eyes and . . . bravely . . . let go!

Laaaaady Miraaaaaanda!

... he thought as he tumbled through the air, hoping for the best.

Ooof!

'Got you!' Lady Miranda exclaimed happily. Pug had landed safely in her arms.

'What about me?!' shouted Arlene von Bling, still stuck.

'Why should we rescue you? How do we know you won't try to steal Pug again? Or any other animals?'

asked Lady Miranda.

'I won't go near another animal,' promised Arlene von Bling.

'Not ever?' asked Lady Miranda.

'Not EVER!' replied Arlene von Bling weakly, throwing her other shoe at an approaching lion.

'Drive up to the fence,' Lady Miranda ordered Running Footman Will.

From the back of the safari vehicle Lady Miranda lifted the sedan chair and propped it up against the fence like a ladder. Pug helped to secure it at the bottom.

'Climb down,' Lady Miranda instructed.

Arlene von Bling hurried down the makeshift ladder.

The curious lions were getting closer and closer. Just as a lion reached out with his paw, Arlene von Bling fell into the back of the safari vehicle.

'Step on it, Running Footman Will!' shouted Lady Miranda.

Running Footman Will did as he was told and they drove off at high

speed with the pride of lions charging after them.

'Give them more picnic!' shouted Lady Miranda.

Pug did his best to help. In the distance, he could see Florence by her mother's side. Pug hoped she liked jam tarts. He was going to miss her.

Lady Miranda took a quick photograph so that Pug would have a souvenir.

* * *

Back at No. 10, The Crescent, Wendy was busy mending the sedan chair.

'How on earth did these claw marks get here?' she asked.

'We met a lion,' said Running Footman Will.

'Several actually,' said Lady Miranda. 'Pug was very brave.'

Pug wagged his tail.

'We also met Arlene von Bling,' said Running Footman Liam, putting the picnic hamper back in the cupboard.

'From that antiques programme?' asked Wendy.

'Not any more,' said Running Footman Will. 'She's been fired!'

'She tried to steal Pug, Wendy,' said Lady Miranda. 'She wanted to sell him.'

'Did she, m'lady?' asked Wendy. 'That wasn't very nice of her.'

'I promise I won't make you meet any more lions, Pug,' Lady Miranda whispered in his ear. 'The safari life isn't for you. And besides, I don't want you having any more nightmares.'

Pug was relieved to hear this. He did enjoy a good night's sleep.

'I'll just have to think of something else you can be,' she added, patting him on the head.